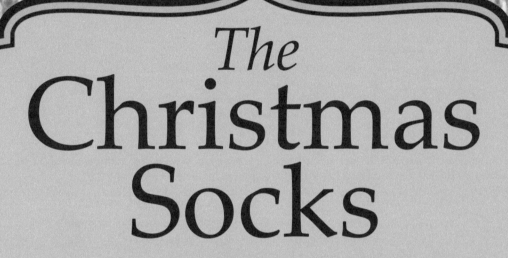

The Christmas Socks

by Douglas Younker

illustrated by Suzette Todd

WestBow Press books may be ordered through booksellers or by contacting:

WestBow Press
A Division of Thomas Nelson & Zondervan
1663 Liberty Drive
Bloomington, IN 47403
www.westbowpress.com
844-714-3454

Interior Image Credit: Suzette Todd

ISBN: 978-1-6642-5373-5 (sc)
ISBN: 978-1-6642-5374-2 (e)

Library of Congress Control Number: 2021925420

Print information available on the last page.

WestBow Press rev. date: 05/27/2022

Who knows how our lives are woven together in a beautiful pattern as we follow our daily to-do list?

The Christmas Socks

Based on a True Story

Do you believe that heaven knows how our individual lives are woven together into a beautiful pattern as we do good deeds for our friends, our families, and even those we do not know? This is a story about getting to glimpse into heaven while helping a neighbor in need.

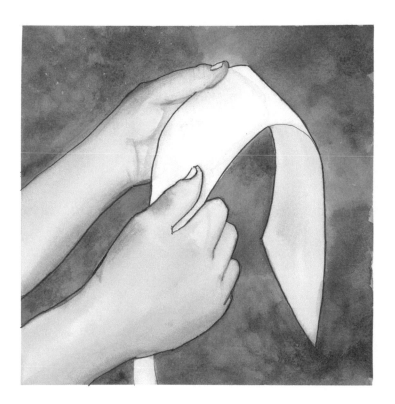

How many of you have a to do list on your fridge doors—things to remember, things to buy, things to start doing, or things to stop doing?

I believe that there is a list of a more divine nature—less tangible but no less real. This is a list of countless messages that trickle down upon us every day from heaven above. He needs us to be His hands here below. Will you help me be one of those helping hands?

If you say yes, then every once in a while, He will let you see a glimpse of the beautiful design He is weaving from the other side.

The Story Begins

Once upon a time, in a land not so far away, there lived two families. One family had a father and three young sons—Jeremy, age nine; Michael; age seven; and Benji, age four.

The other family lived on the far side of town. This family had a father, a mother, and five children. Jesse was twelve; Brittany, eleven; Carson, eight; Hailey, five; and Matthew, the caboose, was two.

With Christmas just around the corner, the stores were full to the rafters with toys and clothes and all kind of goodies, ready for the big holiday.

People were baking wonderful Christmas treats and making all types of holiday candies.

What are you and your family baking or making for Christmas this year? Fill in the blank: (_____)

I hope you will find joy in sharing them with your family and neighbors. Will you?

One of these families wondered whether all the children in their town would have toys under their tree---maybe some new clothes to wear, and good food on their Christmas table.

Which family do you think it was?

The more they thought and the more they wondered, the more they knew that they would do something to help the family that did not have a mother.

They decided to be Santa's secret little helpers.

Have you ever wanted to be a secret Santa helper? I bet you have!

It was a cold and wintery night when they went out into the snowstorm to act as Santa's elves for the family without a mother.

Inside the department store toy aisle, the secret helpers began to ask questions:

"Can we buy Ninja Turtles?"

"I bet they want Transformers."

"Can we get Legos?"

"Let's get 'em basketballs!"

"Well, that's all fine," said the father, "but I bet they'd love some nice, warm socks."

"Socks?" The children looked at their father in shock and disbelief. Brittany, the most vocal elf commented in a very serious tone, "What kind of a Christmas gift is that?"

"Socks are boring," one of the other elves exclaimed.

Another said, "Dad, you can't be serious; no one wants socks for Christmas."

Even with the cries from the elves, the father purchased socks for all the children.

Of course, there were also Ninja Turtles, Transformers, Legos, and other toys in the shopping cart. This made the secret elves very happy, and they quit grumbling about the boring socks.

What types of gifts would you buy? Fill in the blank: (_____).

The helpers also bought a separate basket of food that included a turkey, pumpkin pies, sweet potatoes, stuffing, cranberries, rolls, butter, and a box of candy canes and oranges.

To make it a complete Christmas, the helpers needed to find a Christmas tree. The father knew a man who owned a local tree stand, and when the father asked the man about donating a tree, he was happy to help. Because Christmas was the very next day, the owner wanted those unpurchased trees to be in homes for Christmas.

It was a short drive to the dark and empty tree lot. It was the perfect night to shop for a tree; it was cold and snowing. You know when those big snowflakes fall from the sky, almost like saucers coming down from heaven? Well, that is exactly what it was like. The secret elves scurried here and there, pointing out trees that would be the perfect match.

"It can't be too BIG, or it won't fit in the truck or their trailer home", said one of the elves "If it's too small, it just won't work either. It has to be just right."

There in the far corner of the lot was the perfect tree; it was just the right size, and it had a tag hanging from the snow-covered branch that read, "Noble Fir." Surely this was a sign from above.

With the tree secured in the back of their little red truck, the family of elves were on their way to deliver the Christmas gifts, they could not have looked more Christmas-ier. There was a basket filled with food that would make a wonderful Christmas dinner and provide enough to fill empty cupboards. A second basket was filled with a collection of toys and gifts and, of course, the boring Christmas socks.

The family without a mother lived on a dark and deserted street in a small trailer court on the other side of town. To the elves' good fortune, no one was home when they knocked on the door. Perhaps the other family was out doing their last-minute Christmas shopping. The elves quickly deposited all the gifts on the front doorstep under the awning and leaned the tree up against the side of the trailer. It was a beautiful picture; they inspected their work and felt the falling snowflakes make puddles on their faces as they looked heavenward.

As the elves and their father scrambled back into the little red truck, they anticipated the look on the faces of their secret family as they discovered the baskets left on their doorstep when they returned home. Hopefully, the spirit of Christmas would wrap around them like a warm blanket as it had the secret elves while they were playing

Santa's little helpers. The coldness of the night froze their breaths on the truck windows, but they could not have felt warmer on the inside.

On the way home, they stopped to attend to some of their own last-minute Christmas shopping. The father could not help but think about how blessed they were, and his thoughts kept turning to the young family without a mother. He hoped that their small efforts in some way would bring a little joy to their Christmas season.

At that very moment, a rather untidy and disheveled man crossed in front of the father. Straggling along behind him were three unkempt boys, with tousled hair and raggedy clothing. The father turned and called his boys by name: "Jeremy, Michael, please hold on to Benji so he doesn't get lost in the store."

Caught off guard, the father of the elves stood there with his mouth wide open. Could this be the same little family without a mother?

Father was not the only one who had noticed the uncanny coincidence. The children, those secret elves, looked at each other and somehow knew what they were all thinking.

They watched for a moment and then noticed that beneath each pair of raggedy jeans were three pairs of bare feet, stuffed into worn-out shoes. Yes! Those boring new Christmas socks would indeed be a welcome gift tonight.

The father stopped for a moment and silently thanked the sender of the message for letting his children, the secret elves, be a part of God's handiwork here on earth.

The food, the gifts, the tree, and even those Christmas socks are long gone now, but the warmth of that feeling continues to burn in the hearts of the elves each year when they gather together and remember the year of the Christmas socks.

Now, I have a question for you. Would you be a secret elf this year—one who loves your family, your brothers and sisters, and your neighbors not only at Christmastime but all year long? If you will, shout a big yes!

The End

Epilogue

Years later, one of the secret elves—in fact, it was the same elf who had exclaimed, "Socks are boring!"— was doing a Sub-for-Santa project with her children and found this tag on a Christmas tree at the local department store: "10-year-old boy would like some new socks for Christmas." So yes, Christmas socks make wonderful gifts.

If you would like to be a secret elf this Christmas, gather your family or friends together and pick someone or some family who could be blessed by your efforts, and maybe, just maybe, you will also experience the magic of the season.

Who would you like to help this year? Fill in the blank:

(_____)

The End

Who knows how our lives are woven together in a beautiful pattern as we follow our daily to-do list?

About the Author

Doug was born in Oregon but spent most of his early years in Utah living between Grandparents, a dairy farmer and the other owned a small orchard. He enjoyed working on the farm, milking cows, hauling hay, and picking apples. After college and a 36-year career in the Human Resources field he started his own consulting business helping other HR leaders. He has spoken at many national HR conferences and was invited to speak in Paris, France. Doug is now semi-retired and loves to spend time with his family, skiing, mountain biking and traveling to warm sunny places and to New Zealand where his beautiful wife is from.

About the Illustrator

Suzette Regis Todd is a Bahamian born artist living in the US with her husband and five children. She studied and received a master's degree in Marriage and Family Therapy. She has loved making art her whole life and professes that art is her therapy. She believes we are all connected and that life is all about the relationships. Her greatest joys come from faith, family and friends, and creating.

Printed in the United States
by Baker & Taylor Publisher Services